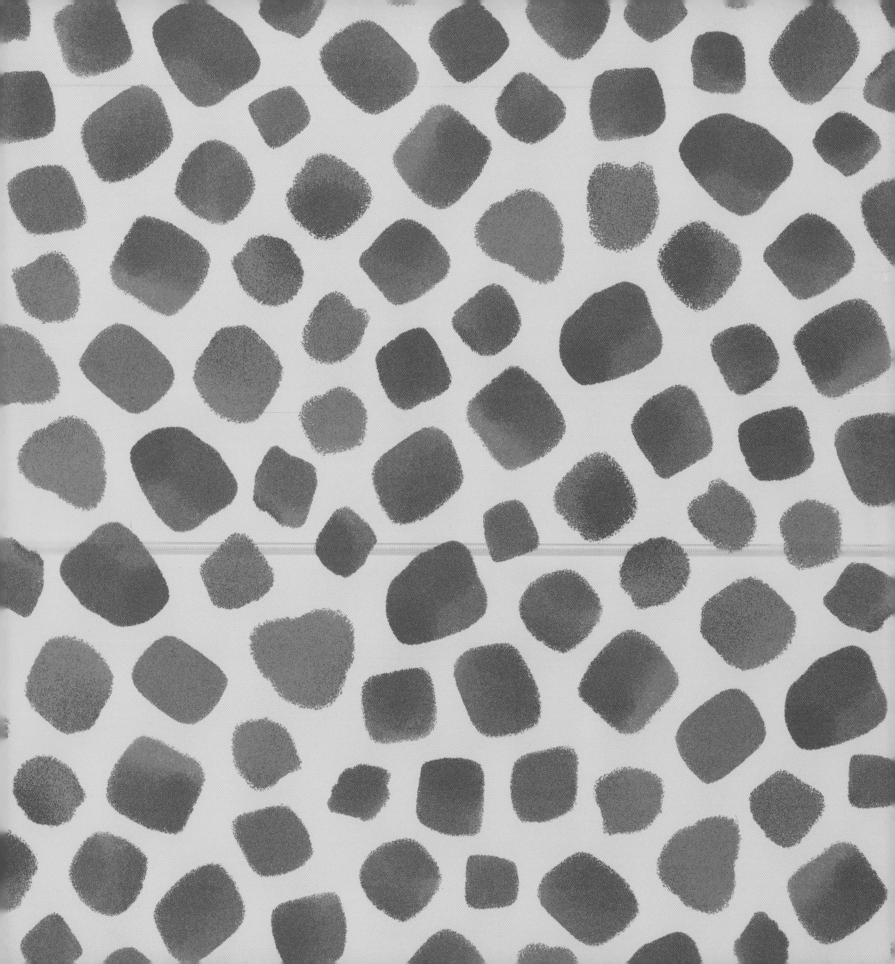

IMAGINE THAT

Licensed exclusively to Imagine That Publishing Ltd
Tide Mill Way, Woodbridge, Suffolk, IP12 1AP, UK
www.imaginethat.com
Copyright © 2019 Imagine That Group Ltd
All rights reserved
6 8 9 7 5
Manufactured in China

Written by Benjamin Richards
Illustrated by Louise Forshaw

ISBN 978-1-78700-909-7

A catalogue record for this book is available from the British Library

'For Mum and Dad'

Little Giraffe's

Far, far away in the African savannah, among the acacia and baobab trees, lived a little giraffe called Gregory.

Every day was the same. Gregory had no one to play with, and he was fed up. He had no giraffe friends, and all the other animals only played with their own kind.

But, one day, Gregory had a big idea ...

Perhaps if he dressed up to look like the other animals, they would let him join in with their games.

So, Gregory set about searching the savannah for the things that he needed.

He searched high up in the trees.

He searched low down in the grass.

He even searched underwater!

Until, finally,
he was ready!

Nervously, Gregory put on his first disguise.

'What kind of fun ostrich games are we playing today?' he asked the ostriches, hopefully.

'You're not a real ostrich, you're a giraffe!'
squawked a noisy ostrich.
'Anyway, you couldn't keep up with us.
You're way too slow!'

Determined to find someone to play with, Gregory put on another disguise.

'Can I play with you?' he asked the rhinos.

'You're not a real rhino, you're a giraffe!' bellowed an angry-looking rhino. 'Anyway, you're not strong enough to wrestle with us!'

But Gregory didn't give up easily, and soon he had put on another disguise.

'Hi, guys, can I swim with you?' he asked the crocodiles at the waterhole.

'You're not a real crocodile, you're a giraffe!'
snapped a mean-looking crocodile.
'Anyway, giraffes are terrible swimmers!'

Giraffes are also very stubborn, and Gregory was no exception.

'Can I join in your game?' he asked the lions,
as he shook his mane and showed his teeth.

'You're not a real lion, you're a giraffe!'
roared a majestic-looking lion.
'Anyway, you're too tall to hide in the grass
and you'll scare away our dinner.'

Gregory thought about giving up, but then he took
a deep breath, and put on his greatest disguise yet.

'Please can I play with you?'
he asked the elephants in
a big, loud voice.

All the elephants turned to look at him.
Gregory smiled hopefully, but one
by one, they started laughing.

'You're not a real elephant, you're a giraffe!'
they trumpeted. 'And you look ridiculous!'

Gregory decided that he'd had enough.

Nobody wanted to play with him.
Gregory had never felt so sad or lonely.

Later that afternoon, Gregory heard a commotion
in the distance. Then he saw something incredible!

The strangest giraffes that he had ever
seen were coming towards him ...

But they weren't giraffes at all!

All of the animals were very sorry for not allowing Gregory to join in with their games and had dressed up to look just like him!

And from that day, the animals of the African savannah always played together.

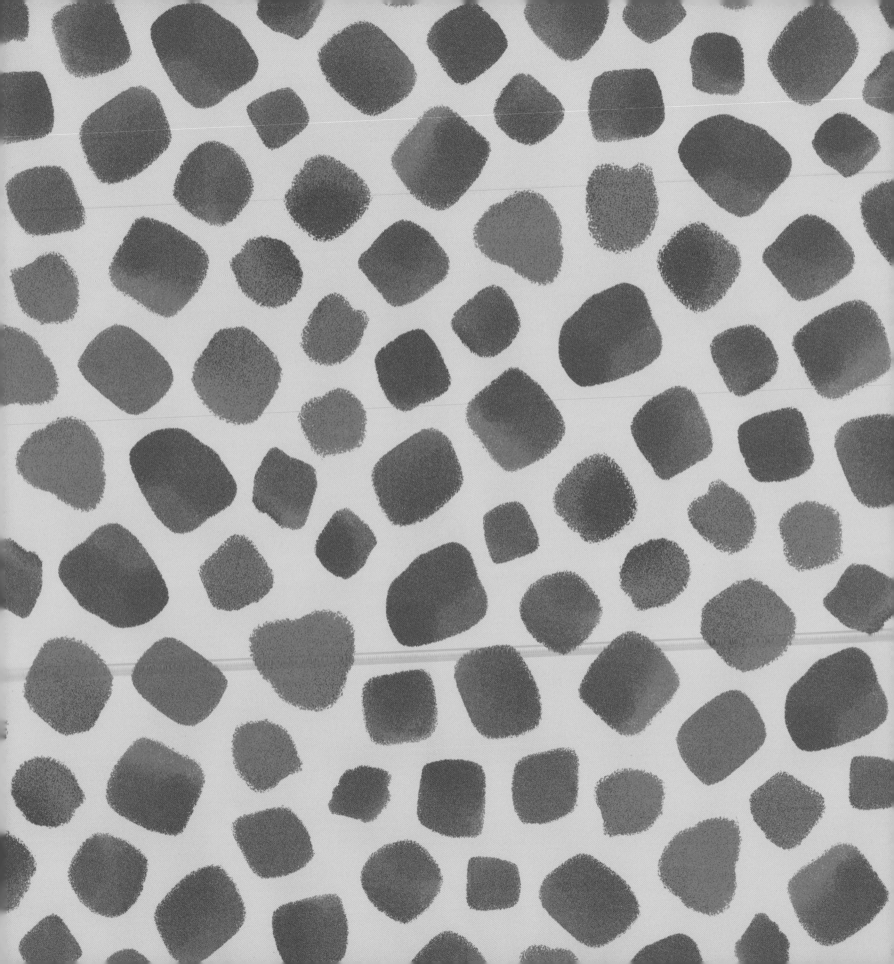